MW01057112

CoW

in the Rain

New Kids Media™ is published by Baker Book House Company, P.O. Box 6287, Grand Rapids, MI 49516-6287

ISBN 0-8010-4503-7

Printed in China

1 2 3 4 5 6 7 – 05 04 03 02

COW
in the Rain

Todd Aaron Smith

GOSHEN PUBLIC LIBRARY
601 South 5th Street
Goshen, IN 46526-3994
219-533-9531

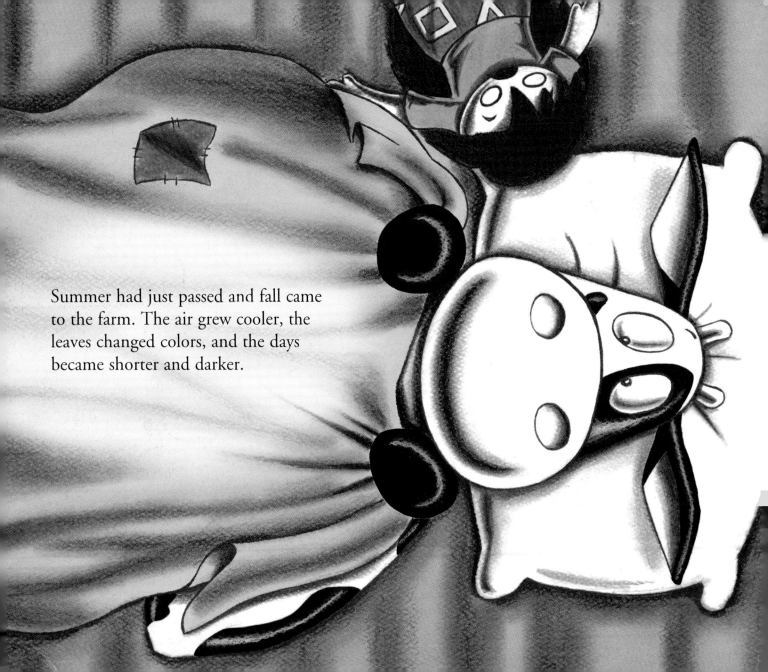

Summer had just passed and fall came to the farm. The air grew cooler, the leaves changed colors, and the days became shorter and darker.

WoOOOooooooo

By night, Cow looked foreward to rest in her snug, warm bed of hay in the barn. But outside . . . "WOOOooo!"
Dog howled at the moon. "WOOOooo"

This made Cow very upset! How could she sleep with Dog's loud howling? What was wrong with him anyway? Cow glared out the barn window. Dog seemed perfectly fine. Loud, but fine. That made Cow angrier.

wOOOOOOOOoooooo

Dog finally noticed Cow at the barn window looking out at him and frowning. Dog was confused. Why didn't Cow say hello? Why did she look so unhappy? Dog stopped howling.

"Hmph!" muttered Cow. "Maybe now that dog will go to sleep like the rest of us!" Cow returned to her warm bed of straw. Minutes later, without warning, Dog began to howl again even louder!

The next morning, Cow complained to Pig: "Oh! That crazy Dog! Do you know what he did? He howled all night. I couldn't sleep a wink. Boy, that makes me angry! I wish that dog wasn't here on the farm!"

Meanwhile, a storm began to move across the plains toward the farm. By afternoon, the sky grew suddenly dark and the wind started blowing harder and harder.

The sky began pouring rain! Pig and the other animals started running toward the barn, and Dog ran into his house to hide. Soon it was raining so hard that it was difficult to see very far.

From way across the field, Cow began moving as quickly as she could toward the barn. The grass under Cow's feet was getting very soggy. EVERYTHING was getting very soggy! Cow knew she had to be careful or she might slip and fall.

On the way to the barn, though, that's just what she did! Cow fell right into Pig's mudhole. SPLAT! The mud was so wet and soft and deep. SLURP! Cow was stuck!

The rain poured down harder and faster, and the mud became even softer until Cow started to sink. "Help me, Pig!" Cow called out. Pig was used to being in the mud himself, but he had never seen a cow stuck in his mudhole before.

Pig, tried to grab Cow's hand, but it kept slipping. "Sorry, Cow! There's nothing I can do. Our hands are too wet. Besides, you're too big and heavy!" With that, Pig ran off to the safety of the barn.

Next Cow saw Horse. "Help me!" Cow yelled. "I'm sinking in the mud. You're strong enough to pull me out!"

But Horse wasn't listening to Cow at all. "Better get out of that mud, Cow!" she neighed, running toward the barn.

Cow was getting very scared now. Just then Chicken ran past. "Chicken!" Cow yelled. "Go get help! I'm stuck!"

"No time now, Cow! I've got to get out of this rain!" screeched Chicken without stopping.

"Now I'm in big trouble!" said Cow, sinking deeper into the mud. "Won't anyone help?" She shut her eyes, wishing the rain would stop.

Suddenly, Cow heard a familiar voice. "Grab on!" it said.

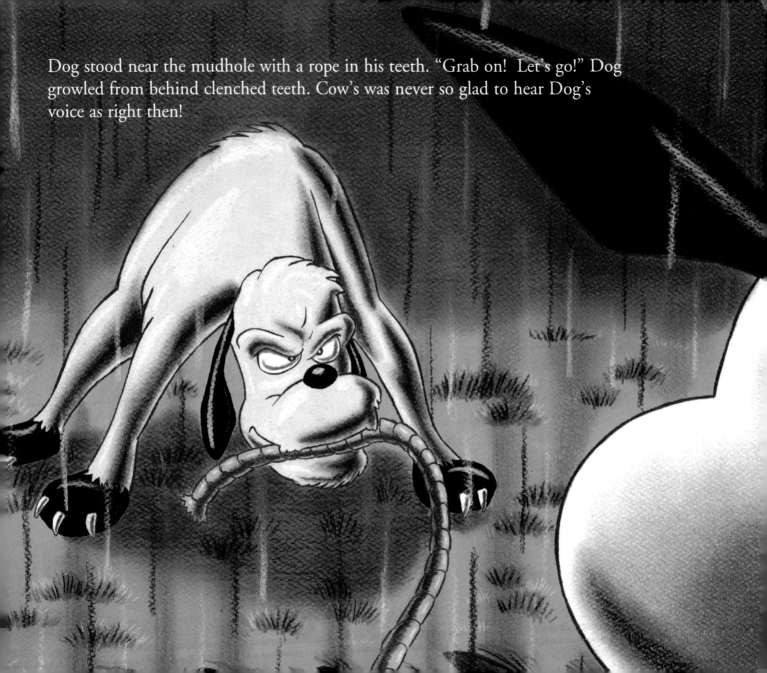

Dog stood near the mudhole with a rope in his teeth. "Grab on! Let's go!" Dog growled from behind clenched teeth. Cow's was never so glad to hear Dog's voice as right then!

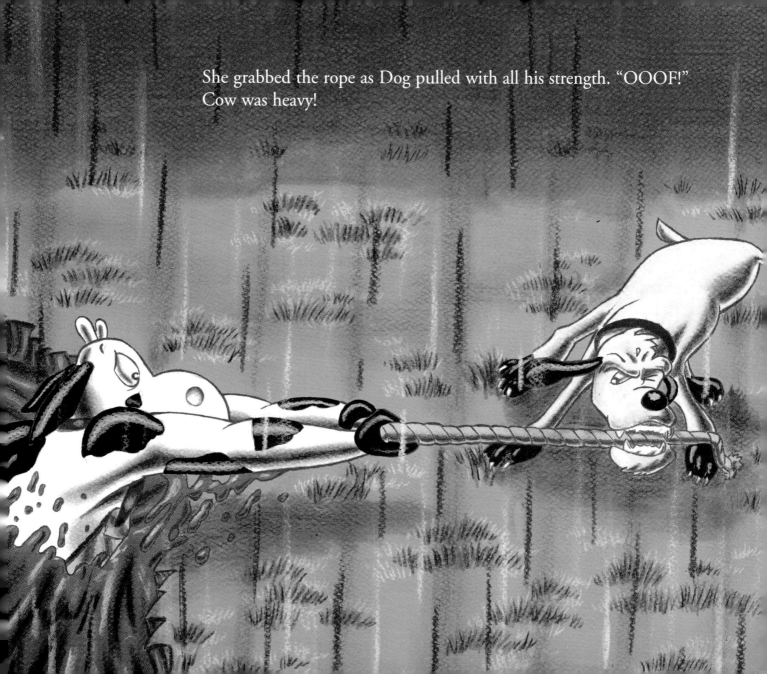

She grabbed the rope as Dog pulled with all his strength. "OOOF!"
Cow was heavy!

SQUISH! POP! Dog pulled Cow out of the mud enough that she could move on her own. She started crawling toward the barn. She was so tired, and so wet and muddy.

Dog continued to pull Cow safely to the doorway of the barn. Then Dog ran back through the rain to his house. Cow didn't have a chance to say anything, even "thanks."

She went straight to her stall. She had been so scared and wet and muddy, but now she was safe in her bed. She listened to the rain hit the roof of the barn and quickly fell asleep.

The next morning, Cow went to visit Dog. "I don't know what to say," Cow said quietly. "My friends wouldn't help me last night, but you came out of the safety of your house to help me. Even after all those bad things I said about you."

"What do you mean?" asked Dog. "Well," said Cow, "yesterday I told Pig that I wished you weren't even here on the farm. Then you were the only one who came to help me when I needed it. You should get some kind of an award!" "Nah," replied Dog. "I don't need a reward for doing the right thing. I'm just glad everyone is safe."

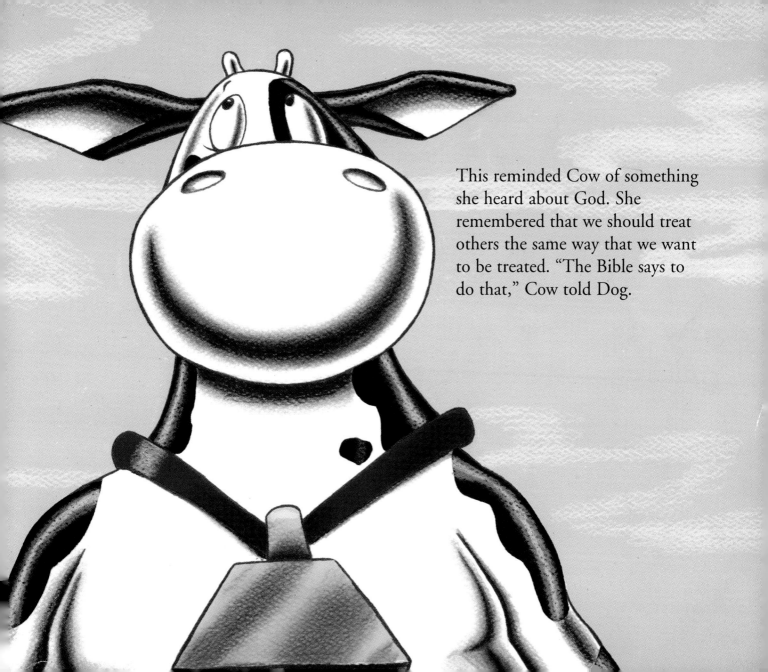

This reminded Cow of something she heard about God. She remembered that we should treat others the same way that we want to be treated. "The Bible says to do that," Cow told Dog.

Cow and Dog spent the rest of the day talking. As it turned out, they had a lot in common. Cow learned that Dog had been howling only because he sensed the storm coming toward the farm. It was a natural thing for a dog to do.

That night all the other animals went to the barn at bed time. But Cow and Dog kept talking softly in the moonlight. They would be friends forever, Cow decided. All because she remembered God's Word. Now on some fall nights, Cow and Dog sit together under the moon and . . .